Fables~
A SHORT ANTHOLOGY

Retold by Janeen Brian
Illustrated by Lisa Herriman
& Lesley Scholes

KEYSTONE
PICTURE BOOKS

A Keystone Picture Book
Produced by Martin International Pty Ltd
South Australia

Published in association with
Era Publications, 220 Grange Road, Flinders Park,
South Australia 5025

Text © Janeen Brian, 1990
Illustrations © Lisa Herriman, 1990
Designed by Lisa Herriman
Typeset by Typecraft, Adelaide
Printed in Hong Kong

First published 1991

National Library of Australia
Cataloguing-in-Publication Data
Fables, a short anthology.
        Includes index
        ISBN   0 947212 65 5.
        ISBN   0 947212 64 7 (pbk.).

        1. Fables. I. Brian, Janeen, 1948-. II.
        Herriman, Lisa, 1962-   .III. Scholes,
        Lesley,1968-   .

398.2

Available in:
Canada from
        Vanwell Publishing Ltd
        St Catharines, Ontario
        (hardcover & paperback)

the United Kingdom from
        Ragged Bears, Andover, Hants.
        (hardcover)

        Arncliffe Publishing.
        Roseville Business Park, Leeds
        (paperback)

Contents

Introduction

Fables are simple, traditional tales with a moral or lesson. They were told thousands of years ago by storytellers, or fabulists, in countries such as Greece and Persia, and were examples of religious ideas and wise or foolish deeds.

Characters in fables were usually animals who behaved as humans. Sometimes people and even natural forces, such as the wind and the sun, were the characters. Animals were given special qualities. The fox was usually cunning; the mouse frail; and the lion, powerful.

Aesop is the best-known fabulist. He is thought to have been a Greek slave, who lived about 600B.C.

Often, people today think of all fables as being Aesop's Fables, even though some were not invented by him. Since Aesop there have been many fabulists such as Sir Roger L'Estrange (1616-1704) and Jean de la Fontaine (1621-1695). However fables have been retold so many times it is often difficult to know who invented them.

Since the beginning of writing, traditional tales have been recorded in books. The fables in this anthology include some well-known and some lesser-known tales. They may be read for their advice, or simply enjoyed as entertaining stories.

THE Fox & the Grapes

One fine day a fox spied a bunch of ripe grapes hanging from a vine. He stretched up, but could not reach the grapes. He ran and jumped, but still he could not reach them. He tried over and over again, then he gave up.

As the fox walked away he said scornfully, "Those grapes may look ripe, but I can tell they are really still too sour to eat."

Some people find fault in what they cannot have.

THE ⬥ Stag at the Pool

A stag, gazing at his reflection in a pool, remarked, "What glorious antlers I have. But my legs are so skinny!" At that moment the stag heard a pack of hunters and hounds approaching. His long legs helped him flee into a thick wood, but his antlers became entangled in the branches. Struggle as he might, he was trapped — and the hounds and hunters closed in.

Sometimes we do not see our own strengths.

THE Young Crab & her Mother

A mother crab was annoyed at her daughter's clumsy way of walking sideways and told her to walk forwards. Obediently the daughter agreed but asked that her mother show her how. The mother began to walk, then realised that she, too, was walking sideways.

Those who live in glass houses should not throw stones.

THE Wolf & the Crane

A wolf had a bone stuck painfully in his throat. He begged other animals to help him and promised a reward. A crane lowered her long, narrow beak down the wolf's throat and drew out the bone. She then reminded him of the reward. The wolf replied that she had taken her head out of a wolf's jaws without being eaten. "That's your reward!" he scoffed.

Don't expect a reward for a good deed.

12

THE Wolf in Sheep's Clothing

A wolf had a clever plan to steal a sheep for his supper. Disguised in a sheepskin, he crept quietly amongst a flock. The sheep suspected nothing. But that night in the farmhouse, the family wanted roast lamb for dinner. In the darkness the farmer mistook the wolf for a plump sheep and took him for their supper.

Pretending to be what you are not can bring trouble.

THE ✦  Ant & the Grasshopper

One autumn day as some ants were busily storing grain for the winter, a hungry grasshopper begged for food. One ant asked what the grasshopper had been doing during the summer while they had been gathering food. "Ah!" he sighed, " I sang all summer long." At this the ant said that he could dance all winter too — and carried on working.

Make hay while the sun shines.

THE ◆ Milkmaid

As a milkmaid walked to market, she dreamt of selling the milk she was carrying, and buying eggs. She planned, when the eggs hatched, to sell the chickens. With that money she would buy beautiful clothes and be admired by all. Just then she tossed her head proudly, and all the milk and all her dreams — spilt on the ground.

Don't count your chickens before they hatch.

THE ◆ Monkey & the Dolphin

A monkey fell from a ship and was rescued by a dolphin. The dolphin asked if he lived nearby. The monkey lied and said, that he did. "Do you know Seriphos?" asked the dolphin. The monkey, thinking Seriphos was a person's name, boasted it was his best friend. As Seriphos was a town, the dolphin knew the monkey was lying, so he dived, leaving him to swim to shore.

Liars give themselves away.

THE  Lion & the Mouse

Once a lion trapped a mouse under its large paw. The mouse pleaded for its life, so the lion let it go. Later the lion became tangled in a hunter's net and roared in distress. The mouse rushed to help. "You're too small to help," said the lion. But the mouse nibbled at the net until the lion was free.

Small friends can be powerful allies.

THE  Fox & the Old Lion

An old lion sent out word that he was ill and that he would like the animals and birds to visit him. Most went but the fox did not. Finally the lion sent for him, asking why he had not come to see him. The wily fox replied, "I had planned to, but I noticed that although many tracks led into your cave, none led out."

Don't just follow the crowd.

THE • Frog & the Ox

A young frog, amazed at the huge size of an ox, rushed to tell her father about the monster. The father frog, trying to impress his child, puffed himself up to look like the ox. The young frog said it was much bigger. Again the father puffed himself up. The young frog insisted the monster was even bigger. The father puffed and puffed . . . and burst!

Pride can be costly.

THE  Wind & the Sun

The wind and the sun argued over who was the stronger. They saw a traveller and agreed that whoever could get the traveller's coat off his body must be the stronger. The wind blew fiercely, but the harder it blew, the tighter the man clutched his coat. Then the sun beamed its warm rays until the man was so hot he took off his coat .

Persuasion is better than force.

THE  Cock & the Jewel

On a farm lived a fine young rooster. He liked to scratch about the hay in the farmyard, where he found insects and titbits to eat. One day his claw flicked up a bright jewel which had fallen amongst the hay. The rooster tossed it aside, saying to himself, "A grain of golden corn would have been better."

Beauty is in the eye of the beholder.

Alphabetical Index